T0208611

In the Dark

Parts 3 & 4

Omid Olfet

iUniverse, Inc.
New York   Bloomington

iUniverse books may be ordered through booksellers or by contacting:

iUniverse
1663 Liberty Drive
Bloomington, IN 47403
www.iuniverse.com
1-800-Authors (1-800-288-4677)

Because of the dynamic nature of the Internet, any Web addresses or links contained in this book may have changed since publication and may no longer be valid. The views expressed in this work are solely those of the author and do not necessarily reflect the views of the publisher, and the publisher hereby disclaims any responsibility for them.

ISBN: 978-1-4401-5811-7 (sc)
ISBN: 978-1-4401-5812-4 (ebook)

Printed in the United States of America

iUniverse rev. date: 07/15/2009

PART 3

Exer's eyes widened in surprise. A headline in the newspaper Exer was reading said a very wild dinosaur was being held in a zoo in a different city. The newspaper story said the dinosaur was so wild and dangerous that il was scaring the visitors very badly. The dinosaur would show his huge sharp teeth and bang against its cage, making visitors fear for their lives. Less and less people were coming to the zoo as a result, and the owner of the zoo didn't know what to do about the situation. The article went on to say if the problem wasn't solved, the owner of the zoo would not be able to afford the expenses of keeping the dinosaur in the zoo.

It had been several years since Exer and his friends had helped the dinosaur and the dinosaur birds return to the Time Tunnel. This new problem shocked Exer, so he decided to talk about the problem with his friends. After much discussion, Exer, Exman, Zoom, and Shelter thought it best to go to the city to see what they could do. Each one of them believed that the dinosaur had to be the same dinosaur whose genes had been stolen from the scientists.

It was a long, tiring trip to the city, but when they arrived, Zoom asked the owner of the zoo if they could see the dinosaur. The owner, who was very mad at the dinosaur for scaring away visitors, told them they could see the dinosaur, and he let them into the zoo. When they arrived at the dinosaur's cage, the dinosaur showed his teeth to Exer and his friends as a sign of anger and made a strange sound.

Omid Olfet

Zoom listened carefully and said, "The dinosaur is very mad at us. He claims he is the previous owner of the zoo in the city where my friends and I are from."

As soon as Exer, Exman, and Shelter heard that, they looked at each other and raised their eyebrows in astonishment. They couldn't believe what the dinosaur was saying!

The dinosaur continued to watch Exer and his friends very angrily and started to throw himself against the cage bars. Zoom said, "How can that be our zoo's previous owner? It's hard to believe."

Exman said, "You are absolutely right. He must be the dinosaur whose genes were stolen. I bet he's lying to us."

"But we should made sure," Shelter said.

"Yes, I agree," Exer said. "How would he know of the zoo in our city otherwise?"

"Maybe somebody told him," Exman offered.

The dinosaur tried to explain how he had become a dinosaur, but Exer and his friends believed the former owner of the zoo was dead. No one had seen him since the dinosaur bird had carried him away, and besides that, they could hardly believe the dinosaur's story about how he had transformed. Swimming in the flooding river and swallowing its water didn't seem very likely as the reason.

"You must be lying," Zoom said.

"You're trying to deceive us," Shelter said.

"But we're smarter than what you think," Exman said. And everybody began to laugh. "You should go and be with your family like the other dinosaur and dinosaur birds. Don't you ever miss them?" Exer asked.

"I've really missed them," the dinosaur replied. "But you should help me be like you again so that I'm able to visit them."

"I thought you just said you were once the zoo owner," Exer said. "That proves you're a liar."

2

"Yes, I am," the dinosaur admitted. "But you didn't believe me. I had to lie so that I could be free."

"You stay here while we think and decide what we should do with you," Zoom said. This did not please the dinosaur, and he showed his teeth again.

The owner of the zoo suddenly yelled, "You had better be nice! If you don't behave, you will not like our decision! I hope you understand that!" The dinosaur made a strange sound again. "What is he saying?" the owner of the zoo asked Zoom.

"He is saying we are all crazy because we are responsible for this situation," Zoom said. "If somebody is crazy it's you!" the owner of the zoo shouted, but his words enraged the dinosaur even more. The dinosaur grabbed the cage bars and tried to destroy the cage. "What are you doing?" The owner of the zoo started to laugh. "Do you think you are strong enough to destroy the cage? You are under my control. I even chose your name, and before you came to me, you were nothing!"

Zoom turned to the dinosaur and said, "That reminds me. I forgot to ask your name."

In his anger, the dinosaur began feeling a strong amount of energy course through his muscles, and he answered very loudly, "POISON!"

The owner of the zoo looked at Zoom. He was very amazed but a little doubtful about Zoom's ability of talking to the dinosaur, so he asked, "What did he say?"

"I asked about his name, and he said it was Poison," Zoom replied.

Zoom's answer convinced the zoo owner that Zoom had real power. "That's right," he said. "That is right."

Exer reminded the zoo owner that they needed to discuss Poison's fate, so the five men began to share their opinions. It was a really difficult task to make a decision about Poison, but in their scheming, Exer and his friends made a mistake. Even the smartest people make mistakes, and in this situation, Exer and friends failed to believe that Poison was actually telling them the truth about his transformation. They refused to accept the fact that Poison was not the dinosaur with human and dinosaur genes.

"So he thinks he used to be a zoo owner, is that right?" the zoo owner asked, and he began to laugh very loudly.

"Yes, that's his lie," Zoom said.

The zoo owner suddenly began speaking to Poison directly. "Poison," he said, "listen to me carefully. I can do whatever I want with you. I can even kill you, so don't even think you are stronger than me. You had better be a good boy and stop frightening the people who come to see you."

Poison did not say anything. As big as ten elephants and still growing, Poison decided it would be best to wait for the right time to make his escape. Meanwhile, Exer and his friends chose to leave Poison in his cage until they were sure he was no longer crazy with anger. If his behavior improved, they would return and make a different decision about Poison's future. Exer and his friends discussed their plan with the owner of the zoo, said goodbye, and returned home.

Poison remained quiet for the visitors and the zoo owner from that time onward. He didn't want the owner of the zoo to hurt him, and he was biding his time until he got the chance to break out and run away. The zoo owner was able to make lots of money again because of Poison's good behavior. He was very happy, but he was not aware of Poison's true intentions. The owner of the zoo thought, "Poison has changed from the way he used to be."

But things are not always the same as they appear.

Everything went back to normal until one very dark night. An earthquake of extreme magnitude struck the area around the zoo where Poison was being kept. The earthquake was so strong that it destroyed all the houses in the area, including the zoo. Most people were caught sleeping at the time of the earthquake and could not escape in time. Many lost their lives, including the owner of the zoo.

The earthquake flattened every building, but nothing happened to huge Poison. At the time of the earthquake, Poison had grown to the size of twenty elephants, and he possessed an enormous amount of power that made him very destructive. With his strength, Poison freed himself, and he stomped around a little while before he ran towards the forest. Poison realized the forest would be an excellent hiding place, and because the earthquake had killed so many people, nobody saw him run towards the forest. When Poison reached the forest, he stepped in between the trees and tried to find a path to follow. He finally found a rough path and ran deeper into the forest.

Exer and his friends heard about the earthquake and agreed to go to the city again and see what had happened to the people and the dinosaur. When they reached the town, the only noises they heard were those of the ambulances looking for survivors who needed to be taken to a hospital. Exer and his friends hurried to where Poison used to be, but they couldn't find him.

"I don't like it here," Exman said. "It looks like everyone has died."

"But where could Poison possibly be?" Exer asked.

"That's a good question, but I don't have an answer," Shelter said.

Exer and his friends looked around for a while, but they couldn't find Poison.

"What should we do now?" Zoom asked.

"I guess all we can do in this situation is wait," Exer said, and they decided to find a place close to the town that was still standing and plan their next move.

Nighttime fell, and a blanket of darkness covered the entire town and forest. During the day time, very little light could penetrate the trees of the forest. At night, it was impossible to see anything, but the darkness didn't bother Poison. He was too strong for any of the animals in the forest to be a threat. But there was one exception.

Omid Olfet

A great black creature with long, sharp teeth and gigantic paws lived in the forest. Its claws and teeth were as sharp as swords, and its eyes shone brightly in the darkness. The creature was aware that there was a newcomer in the forest, so it climbed a tree, perched on a branch, and waited.

One night, Poison was stomping through the forest, and he was very unhappy. His human and dinosaur natures were battling inside him. It was a constant struggle between Poison's two natures because the dinosaur part wanted to escape the human part of Poison's mind that wanted to capture and control the dinosaur. But neither desire was possible. Poison was a strange creature of two opposing natures that could not be separated. He might have looked like a dinosaur on the outside, but underneath, he was partially dinosaur and partially human.

While Poison was stomping around that night, he noticed two bright eyes in a tree. They stared at Poison and never blinked. From its spot among the leaves and branches, the black creature flicked its tail and bared its sharp teeth. The creature was an abnormally large cat—the same cat that had rubbed himself against Exer's wife's skirt! Since that day, he had grown into a gigantic monster, and he was very powerful. The source of his power came from Steeler, but when Steeler died, the cat became the last remaining holder of Steeler's negative power.

Steeler had been the ruler of a different world, but he transferred some of his power to a lightning bug. When a bird ate the bug, it subsequently gained the lightning bug's power. Soon afterwards, a cat ate the bird and grew stronger and stronger with this mysterious power until it became the terrible creature that lived in the forest.

But Poison's power had a completely different source. When the dinosaur from the Time Tunnel ate Melter, he gained Melter's power, which made him able to melt the ice when he left the Tunnel. Melting the ice transferred the dinosaur's power to the water, which caused an enormous river to stream out of the Time Tunnel. Then, when a young man named Max almost drowned in that river, he transformed into a dinosaur as a result. Not long after that incident, the owner of the zoo met the same fate as Max and became Poison.

So Poison was right when he told Exer, Exman, Zoom, and Shelter about his transformation: the water changed him, but it was also the water that gave Poison the power he used against the black cat.

The nature of Poison's power was unique. It was a combination of Melter's positive power and the zoo owner's negative nature. These two forces were always at odds with the other, but the black cat did not have this problem. Because his source of power came from Steeler, the cat was only influenced by a negative nature.

The cat continued to stare at Poison, and Poison stared back. Poison grew very angry and uncomfortable when the cat didn't move. Finally, he grew so impatient that he lost control of his power. The tree that the eyes were staring from fell to the ground. The noise of the falling tree sounded like cannon fire on a battlefield. The crashing sounds and falling leaves filled the air, making it hard for Poison to see anything for a moment. After everything had settled, Poison looked around, not expecting to see the two lights anymore. But he did.

The bright eyes now stared at him from a different tree. Poison's anger began to increase again, and consequently, so did the energy in Poison's muscles.

In his fury, Poison brought another tree to the ground, but this time, he worked faster. The second tree fell quickly, and the leaves littered the ground. When Poison finished the job, he waited for a few moments to see if he made the bright eyes disappear, but just like before, the huge, vicious cat was on a different tree. The black cat was still staring at Poison, and Poison didn't like it.

Each monster knew that the other was incredibly strong, but there was an important difference between the two: the cat was able to climb trees, while Poison could not. Poison realized this, thought for a little while, and then decided to leave the horrible cat alone. "Maybe he's not going do anything to hurt me," Poison thought. "Why am I wasting my energy on him?"

Poison continued going on his way. Poison's greedy, human nature kept nagging him to capture the large cat and put it in his zoo, but his dinosaur nature wanted to leave the cat alone.

These thoughts kept going back and forth in Poison's mind while he stomped across the forest floor. Suddenly, he stopped and looked around. Poison was shocked when he saw the bright eyes again in a tree in front of him. "He must have been chasing me," Poison told himself. "Well, this time I'm going to give him a lesson he'll never forget."

Poison decided to shake the tree the cat was in and see if the creature would fall to the ground. He started to shake the tree, never breaking his eye contact with the bright eyes. Poison watched as the cat jumped to another tree. "If I want to capture the cat, I might have to destroy the entire forest! But there might be thousands of trees in here," Poison thought. "It would be best to just leave him alone and keep doing what I was doing."

Meanwhile, Exer and his friends planned to search for Poison in the forest because that was the only place left to search. The difficulty with searching the forest was that the job required precise planning. It was not an easy task at all. The forest was so big, and they needed lots of equipment to keep them safe and help them find Poison. After a lot of preparation, they arranged everything and were ready to go.

The night before they left, however, something happened.

"Would you please bring me my blue jacket from the closet?" Exer asked his 12-year-old son, Exboy.

"I sure will," Exboy told his father. Exboy went to the closet and opened the door, but while Exboy was taking the jacket off the hanger, something dropped out of the pocket and broke into pieces on the marble floor. Exboy, who didn't expect that to happen, started to panic because he didn't know what to do.

Exer had heard the item break and asked, "What happened?"

After a few seconds, Exboy said, "I don't know. There was a mirror in your pocket."

As soon as Exer heard that, he hurried towards the closet and looked at the pieces on the floor. He looked at his son, who was still holding the jacket in his hands.

"That was my magic mirror," Exer said.

"What did you just say?" Exboy hadn't expected to hear such a thing.

Exer repeated what he had already told his son. "It's not a problem" he comforted Exboy. "Now I can give one piece to each of my friends. I just hope the pieces still work." He helped his son pick up the pieces off the floor, warned Exboy to be careful, and didn't mention the broken mirror again.

The next day, when Exer and his friends were almost ready to go, Exer explained what had happened to the mirror with his friends.

"I hope the pieces have the same power," Zoom said.

"And if they don't?" Exman demanded.

"We don't have another choice," Exer said. "We have to take the risk."

During their conversation, Shelter remained strangely quiet.

"What's wrong with you my friend? Are you ok?" Exer asked Shelter.

Shelter nodded, but he looked a little pale. "I'm all right," he said. Don't worry about me."

"What do you think about the broken mirror?" Zoom asked Shelter.

"Well, if the pieces are still working, we'll have more power because each of us has a piece, but if they don't work, we could be in real trouble," Shelter answered.

Shelter's friends agreed with him, hoped for the best, and said their goodbyes before leaving Exer's house. They had already informed the police of their plan, so they got into the car and drove towards the forest.

By the time they reached the forest, the sun was beginning to set. They knew they would lose the sunlight before they could begin looking for Poison, so they decided to postpone their search until very early the next morning.

Exer, Exman, Shelter, and Zoom got out of the car and organized everything they would need for the next day. They prepared their magic mirrors, guns, grenades, water, food, and their tent before they settled into the tent and went to bed.

Before the sun had risen the next morning, Exer and his friends had already eaten breakfast and packed up their tent. As they made their way into the forest, they decided to stay together and never stray far from the others. Some areas of the forest were open and easy to penetrate, but some areas were densely packed with trees and were not as easy to go through. They walked and walked, with Exer leading the way. They saw nothing but the big, tall trees. After many hours, Exer looked at his watch. It was noon.

"Let's take a rest here for a while before we continue," Exer suggested.

Everybody agreed. They were all very thirsty and tired from the heat and humidity, so they stopped for food and water and decided to rest for a while.

"Where could Poison possibly be?" Exer asked.

"Wherever he is, we'll find him," Exman responded.

"But how long do you think it will take us to find him?" Zoom asked. "We're not even sure Poison is in the forest."

Shelter remained quiet.

"Why aren't you saying anything?" Exer asked Shelter.

Shelter was as pale as he had looked before they left for the trip, and he told Exer that he was not feeling well at all.

"What happened? What's wrong?" Exer asked.

"I'm not sure. Maybe it's food poisoning."

"This is just more bad luck," Zoom groaned. "First, the mirror broke, and now Shelter is sick."

"Would you like to drink some lemon juice? It might make you feel better. I hear it's good for food poisoning," Exman offered.

"Sure, if you don't mind," Shelter said with a very weak voice.

Exman shook his head and gave Shelter some lemon juice. "I hope you feel better."

"I don't think we should waste any more time," Exer said. "Let's go."

Exer and his friends were still a long way from Poison and the black cat. But by the time darkness had fallen, they were very close to the creatures. Now that no sun penetrated through the trees, a scary darkness covered the forest, so Exer and his friends stopped their search for the day. They set up their tent and agreed to get some sleep. The men knew they would not get a good night's rest, but some rest would be better than nothing.

Exer and his friends were so exhausted that they forgot one extremely important thing: sleeping in a place as dark and dangerous as the forest is not always a wise plan. With no one to keep watch, dangerous things could happen without the four friends ever being aware they happened. But the threats of sleeping, the black cat, and the dinosaur were not their only problems. Shelter was not improving at all.

That first night in the forest did not go well for Exer and his friends. They felt uncomfortable not knowing what was happening around them, and they were afraid that something dangerous lurked close by.

On the other hand, the cat did not need sleep and had no fears. He continued to watch Poison eagerly because the dinosaur looked like he wanted to sleep. And Poison did need sleep. He was growing so tired that he almost didn't care about the black monster anymore. Poison fought the urge to sleep, but his eyes kept closing. It took a while, but sleep finally overcame Poison. He closed his eyes and drifted into a deep sleep.

The black cat saw that he had the chance to take advantage of Poison, and he seized the opportunity. When the black monster was sure Poison was asleep, he jumped on Poison's head and clawed out both of his big eyes. The cat worked very quickly—so quickly that the dinosaur didn't even have the time to see and understand what had happened.

Poison, now blind with blood streaming down his face, tried to claw and grasp whoever had attacked him, but the black monster was far beyond Poison's reach. Poison turned around in circles and grew extremely angry, but it was useless. He didn't know which direction to attack.

The black monster, on the other hand, was getting ready for his second attack, but he stopped suddenly when he heard a deafening crash of thunder. Poison was still wandering around blindly, but he also stopped when he heard the thunder. He braced himself for a second attack, but it never came. Both the cat and Poison smelled smoke: Lightening had struck a dead tree in the forest and had started a fire that was spreading rapidly.

Not too far away, Exer and his friends were sleeping in the tent, but when the weather changed, the booming thunder woke them up instantly.

"It's going to rain," Exer said.

"But it was sunny and hot in the day time," Zoom protested.

"The weather is crazy," Exman said.

The only person who did not comment on the weather was Shelter. He was still in his sleeping bag, fast asleep. When Exer, Exman, and Zoom were more awake, they noticed Shelter had not woken up.

"Good for him," Exer said. "I'm glad he slept through the thunder." Exer peeked through the door of the tent. "I don't think we have anything to worry about. It's just a little thunderstorm." Exer explained. "Yeah, there's nothing to worry about, so we don't need to bother Shelter. Let him sleep."

"I agree," Exman said. "Hopefully he'll feel better in the morning."

Exer recommended that everyone go back to sleep, but Zoom kept watching Shelter. "Hey guys," Zoom said, "it looks like Shelter isn't moving at all." Zoom peered closer. "I don't think he's breathing."

Exer gasped. "What did you just say?"

"That can't be right," Exman said.

Exer and Exman drew closer to Shelter's side and looked at him under a flashlight. Zoom put his ear to Shelter's heart and said, "He's gone. We've lost a good man and a good friend tonight." Zoom then checked Shelter's eyes and his temperature. There was nothing they could do for their friend. Zoom guessed Shelter had died about an hour before the thunderstorm had begun. Everybody was shocked and upset.

"What do we do now?" Exman asked.

"We have a serious problem now that he's gone. We've always relied on his help," Exer replied.

Shelter's friends were saddened and frightened that he would not be with them for the rest of their journey. Shelter had always been able to protect them, but now, Exer, Exman, and Zoom had no choice but to continue without him. They buried Shelter and were about to try going back to sleep when all three men smelled smoke.

"Is something burning?" Zoom asked his friends. "Can you smell it?"

"Yes, I can," Exer said.

"I can smell it too," Exman said.

"Is the forest burning?" Zoom asked. He hoped that wasn't the case.

"We need to figure it out," Exer replied.

Meanwhile, the forest fire was advancing, and the smoke was getting thicker and thicker. The battle between the cat and Poison was about to begin again. Poison smashed every tree he came across, but the black monster remained one jump ahead of Poison the entire time. He leaped from branch to branch, always remaining out of the dinosaur's blind reach.

The black cat could no longer get close to Poison because even though the dinosaur was blind, he was so strong in his anger that everything he came across was destroyed. Not a single tree that Poison moved by was left standing.

It was not going to be as easy for the cat to win this time around. Trickery had helped him succeed the first time, but now, the black monster had to carefully situate itself for an attack. The cat leaped from tree to tree to avoid Poison's flailing arms and tail while it waited for the right time to pounce.

As Poison continued to flatten everything in his path, it started to rain. The fire was so fierce that the rain did not help put out the flames. The black monster watched his two enemies very closely. The fire rapidly approached, and Poison continued stomping through the forest, making the ground shake like during an earthquake. Poison could smell the smoke and feel the heat from the fire, but he could not do anything about it. The dinosaur started spinning around because he didn't know in what specific direction to go, and the fire was now so close that it singed his tail.

The black cat watched everything from a tree the fire hadn't touched yet. He wanted to flee, but his thirst for more power kept him from leaving. The horrible monster wanted to kill Poison. If he did that, he would become the strongest creature in the world. The cat remained in his tree a moment longer before his greediness prevailed, and he jumped to a tree near the fire. From there he planned to attack Poison, but as soon as the black monster was ready to strike, an enormous bolt of lightening shot down from the sky and struck the two fighters. Poison and the black monster died instantly, but the lightning combined their powers and shot them up into the sky.

It was not long before their bodies burned in the forest fire—the fire that was now heading towards Exer and his friends. Smoke surrounded the tent where Exer, Exman, and Zoom still slept. Exer woke up, coughing badly because the smoke had finally penetrated the tent. Exman and Zoom soon began coughing as well. The smoke was so thick that the three friends could do nothing but cough. They rushed out of their tent, but there was not enough clear air outside for them to breathe. The combination of the heavy smoke and the rain made it hard for Exer and his friends to find a way to escape the fire, but they soon noticed the flames were too close for them to get away.

Exer, Exman, and Zoom could hardly see one another through the rain and the smoke. Out of desperation, Exer pointed in a direction that seemed to be more free of smoke. The smoke burned their eyes, but with hands over their mouths and noises, the three friends tried to hurry towards the area where Exer was pointing.

As they made their way through the smoke and burning forest, Exer and his friends grew very worried that they would not be able to find a way out. They dodged falling branches and burning trees, but the friends' fear of being trapped only grew. The smoke intensified, which made it more difficult for Exer, Exman, and Zoom to see, and without Shelter, their fate looked grim. Had Shelter been alive, he would have used his power to make a suitable shelter that would have saved their lives. Every one of them wished they had Shelter with them, but they knew he was not coming back. They, themselves, had to find a way to survive.

Exman and Zoom continued to follow Exer, but they were beginning to lose hope. They paused a moment to look around them. They were sweating heavily, they couldn't breathe very well, and worst of all, the fire was surrounding them. The light from fire the fire was so bright that it was almost blinding. Little by little, the fire crept nearer, but it was still not raining hard enough to extinguish the flames.

Not only could Exer and his friends not see each other, but the roar of the fire and the crashing forest drowned out their words. If the friends were trying to communicate, they couldn't tell. Struggling for life, Exer and his friends gathered close together, but they soon realized they had reached their end and stopped struggling. Exer, Exman, and Zoom knew death would bring an end to their close friendship, but they accepted the truth that they had to say goodbye. They gathered together and grasped each others' hands as they lived their last moments. The smoke and heat were unbearable. The smoke filled their lungs and strangled them while the fire eventually burned them all together.

As they died, the thunderstorm continued. Lightening, that was now a combination of Poison's positive power and the cat's negative power, repeatedly shot down from the sky. Poison's power fought against the fire and caused the rain to come down harder and harder. But the cat's power was strong too. It wanted to keep the fire burning, just as Steeler would have wanted. The two forces struggled against the other in the sky. Neither one of them wanted to give up, but the more the cat's power created lightening and fire, the more Poison's power made it rain.

The battle seemed like it would go on forever. By the time the sun set, most of the forest was on fire, but the police and firefighters had arrived to put out the fire. The firefighters flew above the forest in helicopters, trying to extinguish the flames, but they came too late to save the three men in the forest. When the storm would not stop, the firefighters were forced to return to the ground for their own safety. But back down on the earth, the thick smoke made it difficult for the firefighters to search for survivors. They feared the situation was hopeless, but they did their best.

The firefighters continued to risk their own lives as they continued their search for Exer and his friends and as their comrades worked to stop the fire. The search lasted for days, but all they could find in the forest were the ashes of burned trees. They found no clues to lead them to Exer, Exman, Zoom, or Shelter.

The tragic event was the top story on the evening news and the major headline in the newspaper. Everyone from miles around heard about the fire and the deaths. When Exboy and his mother heard the news, they were shocked and couldn't believe such a horrible thing had happened to their loved one and his friends.

"No it can't be right. They must be still alive. They're probably in a shelter somewhere deep in the forest." Exer's wife told this to herself frequently because she knew Shelter was with the group. She was aware of Shelter's power, but she didn't know Shelter had died hours before the rest of his friends. Exer's wife tried to convince her son that Exer was not dead. Exboy prayed and prayed for the safety of his dad and his friends, but he and his mom never heard any news that they had been found.

By the time the firefighters finally put out the entire fire, the whole forest had burned to the ground and everyone lost hope of ever finding Exer and his friends. To comfort Exer's wife, friends and family kept reminding her and Exboy that it was now time for Exboy to take his father's place and become the new hero.

To honor her husband's memory, Exer's wife encouraged her son to be like his dad. Exboy already resembled Exer so closely that almost everybody referred to him as Exer's twin.

So Exboy, who knew the stories about his father very well, promised himself that he would become even smarter and stronger than his dad. Exboy was already a smart child, but he dedicated himself to his studies and began exercising everyday to shape and strengthen his body. Day by day, Exboy grew stronger and smarter.

But before Exboy matured, something strange happened to Exboy that had a significant impact on his destiny. One day while the 13-year-old Exboy was walking through the house, something very sharp scratched the bottom of his foot. Exboy's foot instantly started to hurt, so he sat on a chair to examine the bottom of his foot. Exboy couldn't see anything except for a little blood that was coming out of the cut. He placed a bandage on it so the cut would stop bleeding and began to walk away. But even as he walked, he realized his foot still really hurt. He examined his foot again but did not find anything out of the ordinary. Exboy tried walking once again, but the pain would not go away. Exboy guessed something sharp could be in his foot, so he showed the cut to his mom. She asked what had happened, but she didn't see anything either.

"Just leave it like that then," Exboy said. "It's just a little scratch. Maybe the pain will eventually go away."

"Are you sure you don't want to visit the doctor?" his mom asked.

"Don't worry about it. It'll get better," Exboy said, and they ignored it.

After a few days, Exboy noticed that the pain had not gone away and that his foot hurt a little worse than before. The only noticeable changes were a painful red circle that had developed around the scratch and the fact that Exboy sensed he had more energy and strength. Exboy's mom convinced him he needed to see a specialist to figure out what was wrong.

"Well, this red spot looks very strange," the doctor said.

"Doctor," Exboy said, "It's as red and as hot as fire. It burns."

"I see. Very interesting," the doctor said. "Any other problems?"

"Well, I'm not sure if it's a problem or not, but I started to feel more energy in my body and my mind after this happened to me," Exboy answered.

"Strange," the doctor said. "I think it would be best if I take a sample from the red part of your skin so that I may examine it. Otherwise, I don't have anything helpful to tell you now."

Exboy and his mom nodded in agreement.

"It's going to take about a week," the doctor said after taking the sample.

Exboy and his mom thanked the doctor and returned home.

Back in Exboy's home town and the surrounding area, the battling powers in the sky had not given up their fight. Their struggles caused nonstop raining, which led to horrible flooding. Ever since the forest fire, thunderstorms and rain were much more common. The sun rarely shined, and no one had a good explanation for the problem. The storms came without warning. No one could predict when or where they would hit. The only sign the people had was when the clouds gathered and darkened. The people called the thunderstorm "Roar."

Roar was monstrous and not comparable to other storms at all. Whenever Roar arrived, it would rain heavily for hours and hours, and thunder and lightening filled the sky every minute. The winds blew strongly and destroyed many people's land and property.

As soon as people saw Roar coming, they would pray for Roar not to be sent to them because they feared the dangers and destruction the thunderstorm brought. Roar sent fire and water down to the earth that sometimes proved deadly. The people could only guess that Roar was mad at everybody, no matter who they were or what they had done. What they did not know was that Roar was a fighter—not a regular fighter, but a powerful one who was a combination of two monstrous fighters with tremendous power: the black cat and Poison.

As Roar continued to terrorize the people, Exboy waited anxiously for the week to pass. When the time came, Exboy rushed to the doctor's office. He was very eager for the results.

The doctor's news was completely unexpected. "Based on my examination last week and what I have learned from your skin sample, you seem to have a sharp particle in your foot," the doctor said, "but this particle is very strange."

"Why?" Exboy asked.

"Unfortunately, as long as it is in your body, I won't be able to understand the true nature of the particle," the doctor explained.

"Well, why don't you pull it out and look at it?" Exboy asked.

"That's the point. We never seem able to have everything we want at the same time, now do we?" the doctor asked.

"Doctor, I don't understand. What does that have to do with the stuff in my foot?" Exboy asked.

"Be patient. I'll tell you," the doctor said. He cleared his throat and looked at Exboy very seriously. "This sharp particle is giving you a superpower."

"What? A superpower? What kind? I still don't understand," Exboy said.

"A superpower of the mind," the doctor explained, but after he said that, he suddenly looked a little sad. "Do you still want to keep that particle in your body?"

"Yes, yes, yes! I sure do," Exboy said excitedly.

"Well, that's the good news. Now you have to hear the bad news," the doctor said.

"What do you mean?" Exboy asked.

"I mean if you keep the particle in your body, you will have a bad infection around the cut," the doctor explained. "I'm afraid the infection will be very painful, and then it will spread all through your body. It'll start from your cut, cover your foot, and then move up towards your head."

"Then what?" Exboy whispered.

"Very simple. The infection will eventually reach your stomach, intestines, bladder, kidney, lungs, and finally, your heart," the doctor said. "And then," he hesitated a moment before continuing. "You will die." Exboy's eyes widened. "But the speed of infection will be very slow. It might take years and years before it becomes fatal."

Exboy looked down at his hands and went into deep thought.

"Now it's up to you. You must decide whether you want to keep the particle in your foot," the doctor said. "You have to choose between life without the power or life with it and the fatal infection."

Exboy was completely astounded by what the doctor was telling him. He shook his head and said, "It can't be right. How is it possible?"

"I have told you nothing but the truth," the doctor answered.

"I should think about it carefully, and then I'll tell you my decision," Exboy said.

"That's a good idea, but let me tell you one last thing: every infected part of your body will need to be removed," the doctor said.

"So you mean, if I decide to keep the particle in me, I will lose my fingers, feet, legs, and so on...little by little...is that right?" Exboy asked.

"That's exactly right," the doctor said.

"I'll think about it," Exboy repeated. He wished the doctor a good day, and with his thoughts spinning, Exboy returned home.

It was a difficult decision. After he had talked to his mom about the situation, he was able to guess what was in his foot: a tiny piece of the magic mirror he had broken. When the glass had shattered on the hard floor, a piece must have been so small that they hadn't noticed it. And now, it was in Exboy's foot. Exboy realized it had to be the source of the superpower, and he had to decide if it was worth his life to keep the piece of mirror within him. He weighed his options very carefully and considered the consequences of either choice.

After several days, Exboy finally decided to keep the sharp particle in his foot.

"There are a lot of enemies out there," Exboy told the doctor. "And if I am supposed to be anything like the hero that my father was, I will need every advantage."

"What could possibly be so dangerous for a young boy like you?" the doctor asked.

Exboy told the doctor about his father and what Exer had set out to do before he had died. "But you can't be sure Poison is even still alive," the doctor argued.

"I know that. I will have to be careful," Exboy said, "but if I don't do anything, I would be putting my life, my mom's life, and everyone else's lives in danger. Poison is very dangerous. I have to learn what happened to him."

"I suppose you're right," the doctor said. "It's your choice. Just be careful and make sure you budget your time. If this takes too long, the infection will kill you first."

"Yes, I will keep that in mind," Exboy promised. "If I don't, there will be no point attempting what I want to do. Thank you for all your help, Doctor."

Exboy said goodbye to the doctor. He was grateful the infection would be slow, but that didn't mean Exboy had time to waste. He had to be very careful and use his time wisely. He was not sure about Poison's location, and he definitely did not know whether he was alive or not.

Exboy remembered his father explaining the misunderstanding regarding Poison. Many believed the dinosaur was actually the one that had been created from the human and dinosaur genes stolen years ago. No one realized the dinosaur whose genes had been combined was actually in a city many, many miles away.

But the threat of a dinosaur was not as frightening as Roar. Exboy had never heard of the horrible thunderstorm until he saw Roar mentioned on the news. Since there had been no new information about Poison, Exboy decided Roar should be targeted and destroyed first. Roar was causing too much devastation and fear. Even though the nature of Roar's power confused Exboy, he knew Roar had to be stopped.

Exboy soon realized his job of fighting Roar would be extremely difficult. Just like everybody else, he didn't know where Roar was coming from, he didn't know when he was coming, and he did not understand the nature of Roar's power. From the stories he read and heard about Roar, Exboy discovered that Roar was coming from the sky, but he didn't understand how. "Roar could be a machine," he thought. "A normal thunderstorm with lightning is never as destructive as Roar is. So maybe he uses a machine to create his terrible storms." Exboy continued to ponder that possibility, but Exboy could not figure out a way to predict when Roar would come. The nature of Roar's power bothered Exboy as well, and that above all else was the problem he wished he could solve first. Otherwise, Exboy had no way of knowing how to equip himself so that he could destroy Roar.

Exboy decided the best thing he could do was wait for Roar to come. That way, he could see Roar for himself and figure out if there was anything he could do about the situation. He did not know when Roar would strike again, and he felt uncomfortable doing nothing while he waited. To fix that problem, Exboy decided to work on a top-secret project he had been thinking about. It would be tough and time consuming, but he knew it could possibly help him battle Roar.

Exboy wasted no time in starting his project. By the time he had finished, Exboy hoped to create a deadly, fighting robot that could not be destroyed. Exboy called his robot Risco and did not tell anyone about his creation. Exboy used his father's wealth to help him build Risco and to hire a team of the smartest scientists and engineers to help him finish the project. Exboy's dream of an unbeatable robot would need a large amount of time and effort to come true, but he never gave up. Exboy believed he would be able to destroy his enemy before the infection destroyed him.

In a different city far away from Exboy, a monstrous creature was growing up. Under the care of a greedy doctor, Stinger was well fed and grew bigger each day. The doctor kept telling himself that being a doctor made him a rich man, but he could become an extremely wealthy man if he displayed a dinosaur in a zoo. He made all the arrangements for Stinger to be put in a cage at the local zoo and then asked his son if he would like to visit.

"Yes, Daddy!" his son answered excitedly. "I love the zoo!"

When they got ready, they stepped out of the house, got into the car, and drove to the zoo. They soon made their way to the cage that Stinger occupied.

"Do you like him?" the doctor asked.

His son was a little frightened by the large animal, but he said, "Yes. What is that?"

"That is money," the doctor answered.

"Money? What do you mean, Daddy?" the doctor's son asked. "I was talking about the animal in the cage."

"Oh, I'm sorry," the doctor answered. "He's my little boy."

"Little boy?" The doctor's son was even more confused. "Your little boy is me."

"Oh my son, I'm so sorry. I must be bad at explaining things," the doctor said.

"That's ok, Daddy," the doctor's son said. "But you still haven't told me what kind of animal that is."

"Well, his name is Stinger," the doctor said, but when his son didn't say anything, he wondered if his son had completely forgotten everything about the dinosaur. It had been a long time since his son had named the dinosaur, but as soon as the doctor's son heard the dinosaur's name, his memory began to search for why that name sounded so familiar.

"It looks like you are thinking about something. Are you all right?" the doctor asked.

"Yeah, I'm ok," the doctor's son answered, and he kept trying to understand what was nagging at the back of his mind. The answer seemed to be on the tip of his tongue, but the more he tried to figure it out, the less he could remember.

"Isn't he amazing?" the doctor asked.

"Yes, he is," the son answered.

"We will be very rich," the doctor said.

"How rich?" the son asked.

"We'll be millionaires," the doctor replied, smiling.

"Wow," the son said.

"Would you like to pet him?" the doctor asked his son.

His son did not like the idea of petting the scary creature, so he said, "No, Daddy. That's ok. Let's go."

"Are you sure? He's not going to hurt you," the doctor said.

"I'm sure," the son answered, and they went back home. The doctor's son tried to remember why Stinger seemed so familiar all the way home and throughout the rest of the day, but he had no luck.

One very dark night, the doctor's son had a nightmare about Stinger. The doctor's son called to the dinosaur by name. "Stinger, Stinger," he repeated. The dinosaur's eyes glowed when he heard his name, and when the doctor's son called to him again, Stinger's eyes shone brighter than before. Stinger showed his sharp teeth, and the doctor's son called to him one last time. Stinger didn't move, but an incredible brightness shined in front of the boy's eyes. He instantly woke up, screaming very loudly. The doctor heard his son's screaming and hurried to his room.

"What happened? What happened?" the doctor asked.

"I had a scary dream, Daddy," the doctor's son cried.

The doctor tried to calm his son. "It's ok, it's ok," he whispered. When his son continued to cry the doctor asked, "What did you dream about?"

"I saw Stinger. His eyes were as bright as fire," the doctor's son said. "It was so scary. Daddy, tell me more about Stinger. Who is he?"

"Don't worry about him. It was just a nightmare. Stinger will bring us good luck. You'll see," the doctor said. "Sleep tight. You have to go to school tomorrow." The doctor smiled at his son and turned off the light as he left.

In the morning, the doctor's son could still remember the nightmare. His dad took him to school but didn't bring up Stinger at all. The doctor was very ashamed with himself; he didn't want to tell his son the truth. He thought of that day so many years ago when he had asked his son, "If you had a dinosaur, what name would you choose for him?" His son had responded with the name "Stinger," but when his son then asked the doctor why he had asked him such a question, the doctor's response had been a lie: "I wanted to see how strong your imagination is." Because he hadn't told his son the truth, the doctor now felt very guilty, but he refused to tell his son about his lie.

After school had ended that day, the doctor's son told one of his closest friends about the nightmare.

"Do you know somebody who can interpret dreams?" the doctor's son asked his friend.

"Yes! My grandpa can help you," his friend answered.

"Is there anyway that I can meet him?" the doctor's son asked.

"Probably, but we'll have to arrange a good time for you to come over," his friend said.

"Ok. We'll talk about it tomorrow," the doctor's son said, and they went home.

The next day, the doctor's son met his friend again. "Did you talk to your grandpa about me coming over?" the doctor's son asked.

"Yes I did," his friend answered. "How about 7 'o clock tomorrow night? You can pretend that you need my help on your homework."

"Perfect! I'll talk to my dad about it."

Like they had planned, the doctor's son pretended he needed to see his friend for some help on his homework. The doctor was busy and didn't have to time to help his son, so he said, "That's fine, but don't come back late." "Ok, Daddy," the doctor's son promised, and he left for his friend's house, which was close to his. Once he had arrived, the doctor's son rang the bell. His friend opened the door and led the doctor's son to a small room. An old man was sitting by a fireplace. To the young boy, he looked like he was 90 years old. "Hi," the doctor's son said to the old man.

"Hello my son," the old man answered weakly. "Have a seat." He pointed to a chair close to him. "I hear you and my grandson are good friends," the old man said.

"Yes, Sir, we are," the doctor's son replied.

"My grandson has told me about you and your nightmare, but I want to hear it from you," the old man said. "Tell me exactly what you saw in your nightmare."

"Yes, Sir," the doctor's son said, and he told his friend's grandfather everything he could remember about his nightmare.

When he finished, the old man looked into his eyes very deeply and said, "Everything in this world has a name. Am I right?" he asked.

The doctor's son didn't know why the old man was asking him this, but he answered, "Yes, Sir."

"What is your name?" the old man asked.

"Sam," the doctor's son answered. "But what does that have to do with my nightmare?"

"I will tell you all in good time, my son," the old man answered. "Now, if you don't have a name, what would people call you?" the old man asked.

"I don't know, Sir," Sam responded.

"Exactly, Sam! Your name is your identity. It is everything you are and that includes your power and intelligence. Without a name, you are nothing. Do you agree?"

"I guess so," Sam said, but he wasn't really sure.

"Now, I want to tell you something about that monstrous creature you call Stinger. Are you ready?" the old man asked.

"Yes. Yes, I am," Sam answered repeatedly.

"There is something lurking in the back of your mind about Stinger. You used to know something very important about him, but you cannot remember that now. Am I right?" the old man asked.

Sam was surprised at the old man's accuracy and answered, "Yes. How do you know that?"

"I interpret dreams, Sam," the old man answered, and then he grew very serious. "Now, if you remember whatever it is you are trying to remember about Stinger, you will unlock his power, which would allow him to destroy the whole city and kill everybody," the old man said.

As soon as Sam heard that, his heart started beating rapidly and his eyes widened.

"How badly do you still want to remember everything?" the old man asked.

"Not at all," was Sam's frightened answer.

"That's a good lad," the old man said. "But as soon as you do remember Stinger, everyone could be in real danger," the old man warned.

"What should I do now?" Sam asked.

"Don't try to remember anything about that monster," the old man replied. "His power is sleeping at the moment, but if you remember him, you will wake up his power."

Sam was very scared by the old man's warnings, but he thanked his friend's grandfather and got up to leave. While he was stepping out of the house, he heard the old man give one last piece of advice:

"Be sure to remember that calling the monster in your nightmare made his eyes glow, so don't say his name in you mind. You are the key that will unleash his power. Don't let him go free."

"I won't," Sam promised, and he left for home.

The next day, Sam's father asked him if he would like to play chess with him.

"Yes, Daddy. I love playing chess with you."

In the middle of the game, Sam moved his king to a dark square. The doctor said, "Don't move your king there. That's a dark square."

"What's wrong with that?" Sam asked.

"Use your imagination."

As soon as Sam heard the word "imagination," something echoed in his memory. *Imagination, imagination, imagination.* Sam realized his memories of Stinger were coming back, but he didn't want to remember anything. He grew very scared because the more he remembered Stinger, the more there seemed to be a connection between him and the dinosaur. Suddenly, Sam heard the monster begin making angry sounds, so Sam told his memories, *Get out of my mind! I don't want to remember about you!* And Stinger grew quiet.

"Did you say something?" the doctor asked.

"No," Sam answered. "Let's get back to the game."

"Alright. Now, where were we? Oh yes, I was talking about imagination," the doctor said.

PART 4

"Look at that dark cloud, Mom. Does it look like an eye to you?" Exboy asked.

"Yes, it's kind of strange," his mom replied.

A few minutes later, a bright flash of lightning shot down from the middle of the eye-shaped cloud, and a tremendous peal of thunder immediately followed.

"We better go inside. It's going to start raining soon," Exboy's mom said.

"Inside where?" Exboy asked with a mischievous glint in his eye.

"What do you mean, inside where? Where else would we go but inside the house?""Well, do you want to go in my house or your house?" Exboy asked.

"We only have one house," his mom reminded Exboy. "What in the world are you talking about?" She cast a suspicious glance over her son and waited for his answer.

"I have a surprise for you. Would you like to see it?" Exboy asked.

This was not the response Exboy's mom had expected, but she nodded and agreed she would see Exboy's surprise.

Exboy whispered something that Rose thought sounded like a magical incantation. After a few seconds, an incredibly large machine appeared on the ground. The machine was as big as a wide, multi-story house with a large number of bright windows.

Exboy's mom could hardly believe what she was seeing. She rubbed her eyes vigorously for a while to make sure she wasn't imagining the machine's existence, but when the machine never disappeared, she was at a loss of anything to say except, "What is that?"

"After several years of hard work, my dream has finally come true," Exboy said. "With this machine, I will be able to destroy all those who threaten the lives of others."

"But that just looks like a house to me," his mother protested.

"Well, it may look like a house right now, but it can transform into a deadly weapon very quickly," Exboy said.

"How did you make such a thing?"

"That's a long story," Exboy answered hastily. Changing the subject, he said, "You didn't tell me if you wanted to go inside or not."

His mom let her gaze drift up and down her son's creation. Not only was she amazed by the size and capabilities of the house, but she was stunned at her son's abilities to create such a machine. "I do," she breathed and smiled at Exboy.

Exboy whispered something again, and a vast door opened, permitting them to enter the machine. When they crossed the threshold, the entry door closed automatically behind them. Exboy's mom looked at the door for a second and turned her head back around quickly.

"Don't be nervous, Mom," Exboy said soothingly. "I know you have lots of questions, but don't worry. All will be explained later."

The pair had barely stepped away from the door when Exboy's mom saw a big, muscular man coming towards them.

"Who is he?" Exboy's mom whispered.

"Mom, let me introduce you to my assistant," Exboy said.

"How are you doing ma'am?" the man said. My name is Rockman."

"A pleasure to meet you Rockman. My name is Rose," Exboy's mom said.

"It's very nice to meet you," Rockman said. "Let me show you your room." He gestured for Rose to follow him and then led her and Exboy through the house.

"Exboy, this is all lovely, but when will we return to our house?" Rose asked as they made their way down a long hallway.

"I wouldn't worry about that right now, Mom," Exboy said. "Besides, we have to at least wait until the storm has passed." They walked a few more paces before the party stopped in front of a closed, wooden door. Exboy took a key from his pocket and unlocked the door. He stepped aside for Rockman to open the door. Exboy and his mom walked in, and Rose's jaw dropped. The room was decorated very beautifully. Rose was so amazed she didn't say a word. "It's all for you, Mom," Exboy said, and they hugged each other. But before Exboy could show his mother around, a warning came over the intercom: "A Target is found. A Target is found. A Target is found."

"I have to go," Exboy said.

"Where are you going?" Mom asked.

"I need to attend to that warning. I'll be back as soon as I'm done," Exboy said. "Oh, and if you need any help, just press the assistance button." Exboy and Rockman said their goodbyes and rushed to the computer room.

The computer room acted as the brain of the machine. No one was allowed to enter except for Exboy and Rockman. They were the only people trained to work the complicated systems on the computers. Each door required a different password before entry, so Exboy entered the appropriate code and went inside. Rockman instantly went to a computer at the back of the room and began watching the monitor. Rows of computers lined the large room, and cameras monitored every inch of the area. Additional equipment and technological devices filled much of the empty space.

"There he is," Rockman said while pointing at his monitor. "He came back again."

"Who is he?" Exboy, who had sat next to his friend, asked.

"I'm not sure," Rockman said.

"Have you told the computer to research the target?" Exboy asked.

"No, I haven't yet, but I'll do it now," Rockman said, and he typed a question on a nearby computer. Information instantly appeared on the monitor. Exboy began reading over Rockman's shoulder and felt a strange sense of satisfaction when he read that the target was a super strong creature by the name of Roar.

"Do a background check," Exboy instructed.

In response to Rockman's query for a background check, the system explained that Roar's energy had a complicated nature that gave the appearance of there being a combination of two power forces. "The computer shows that Roar has been behind many crimes in the past, including the floods that have destroyed so many houses and killed hundreds of people," Rockman said.

"Set up the system to be on alert and program the saving component to capture Roar's power and contain it," Exboy said.

"Yes Sir," Rockman said and fulfilled Exboy's orders. He felt confident that Risco's saving component, which was an enormous panel built to contain unfathomable amounts of energy, would be strong enough to hold Roar.

Exboy and Rockman waited for Roar to appear. The sky was completely black, but all of a sudden, Roar came into view. Exboy shouted for the saving component to be activated, and in a short span of time, all of Roar's energy was absorbed by the saving panel. A smile of victory appeared on Exboy and Rockman's faces, but the happiness didn't last long. A different warning suddenly echoed throughout the computer room: "Power limit surpassed. Power limit surpassed. Power limit surpassed."

"What does that mean?" Rockman asked nervously.

Exboy cleared his throat. "It means Roar's power is too great for Risco to handle. This isn't..." but Exboy was cut short when a new warning came over the intercom: "Power limit surpassed. We're about to take off. Power limit surpassed. We're about to take off. Power limit surpassed. We're about to take off."

"And what does *that* mean?" Rockman asked, more angrily this time.

"We're going up," Exboy said. Worry was etched into his face.

"Can't we do something?"

"I'm not sure," Exboy said. He stared out the window as Risco rapidly began rising into the air.

"Wouldn't it be better to let Roar go free before it's too late?" Rockman suggested.

"No. I refuse to let him go," Exboy stated.

"So you're willing to let us all die in space?" Rockman stood up and faced Exboy, scowling deeply.

"Risco was built to withstand all environments imaginable. This machine has many capabilities, so this will be an excellent opportunity to try them," Exboy said. Rockman opened his mouth to protest, but Exboy said, "Let's disappear and see what will happen," Exboy said.

"I don't think it'll help us. All of Risco's power is being used to manage Roar," Rockman said.

"Don't panic. The enemy is under control," Exboy said calmly. "Push the disappear button."

Rockman shook his head in disbelief but pushed the button. Risco disappeared. Any onlooker could no longer see Risco, but the passengers were still able to see one another and everything within the machine. After a several minutes, Exboy pushed the appear button and asked the system about their location. The machine repeated, "We are in space. We are in space. We are in space."

Rockman turned to Exboy and growled, "I told you to let Roar

Omid Olfet

go free, but you didn't! And now it's too late! If we stop, we'll fall down and die!"

Exboy remained calm and didn't look at his friend. Instead, he focused on altering the setup for Risco's entire system. All the controls and functions were still working appropriately, but Exboy realized he had no control over Risco's ascension. For the time being, they would have to allow Risco to keep its course because stopping the machine would only result in their deaths. Exboy decided to check Risco's saving room to make sure everything was still operational. He peered through the window on the room's door and immediately lowered his gaze. Roar's power was sparkling so brightly that the light was almost blinding.

Before Exboy returned to the computer room, he visited his mother. She had been watching TV at the time Risco was rising, but the television had quickly gone off when Risco broke through the atmosphere. Rose tried to change channels and checked to see if something wasn't plugged in correctly, but it was useless. Rose pushed the assistance button just as her son entered the room.

"Is everything all right, Mom?" Exboy asked.

"The TV stopped working," Rose said. "I don't know why it won't turn back on."

Exboy realized his mother wasn't aware Risco was currently in space, so he said, "Don't worry about anything, Mom. We'll fix it, but in the meantime, let's go to the garden and look at the flowers. I think you'll be impressed."

Rose accepted the offer eagerly, but asked, "When are we going to go back home? I have lots of things to do."

"Yes, I know," Exboy replied. "We will go home soon."

Exboy led the way to the garden, and as soon as Rose saw the beautiful flowers, she took a deep breath and smiled. "What a beautiful garden," she said. "It looks like heaven." Rose noticed an area completely covered with roses and began walking towards the beautiful flowers.

"This place is just for you, Mom," Exboy said. Rose gave a small smile before suddenly bursting into tears. "What's wrong, Mom?" Exboy asked. "I thought these roses would make you happy."

"I'm ok," Rose said. She gently touched a rose petal and sighed. "Life is too short. I can still remember the roses your dad used to buy me for my birthdays. He would always tell me that I was more beautiful than any rose."

"Don't be sad, Mom," Exboy said. "Dad is in a better place now, and he wouldn't want us be sad." Exboy gave his mom a hug. He was about to show her the rest of the garden when Risco sent out another warning: "Shortage of oxygen. Shortage of oxygen. Shortage of oxygen."

As soon as Rose heard the warning, she asked her son, "What's wrong?"

Exboy tried to act as though everything was fine, so he told his mom, "Don't worry about anything. With air pollution being such a problem nowadays, something must be clogging the air filter. That must be why the machine is warning us. Everything is going to be fine. Don't worry," Exboy repeated.

"This is such a strange machine. First the TV doesn't work, and now there's a shortage of oxygen. What next?" Rose said.

"Shortage of oxygen cancelled. Shortage of oxygen cancelled. Shortage of oxygen cancelled," the machine repeated a few minutes later.

Exboy grinned. "I told you there was nothing to worry about." Rose raised her eyebrows as if she didn't quite believe her son. Exboy gave a small cough and tried to divert his mother's attention. "Well, I think it's time you went back to your room, Mom," Exboy said. "There's lots of important things that need my attention."

"Very well, but may I stay here a little longer and enjoy the flowers?" Rose asked.

"I would rather you be in your room, Mom. It's the safest place for you right now," Exboy stated.

"Why? Will something happen if I stay here a little longer?" Rose asked suspiciously.

"Mom, I'm just worried about you because I love you so much," Exboy confessed. "But if you would like to stay here for a while, I won't stop you."

"Oh, Exboy," Rose said as she tried to hold back her tears, "you are everything to me. Thank you so much for letting me stay here." Rose hugged her son very firmly, but Exboy cried out in pain.

"What happened? Did I hurt you?" Rose asked anxiously.

"I forgot to take my medicine," Exboy admitted.

"You should be more careful," Rose said sternly.

Exboy pulled his medicine from his pocket and did not hesitate to swallow the pain reliever.

"This pain is killing me, Mom," Exboy said.

"Oh sweetheart, I'm so sorry. Don't you think you should have let the doctor get the particle out of your foot?" Rose asked.

Exboy looked at the slightly bigger red, infected spot before answering, "I don't think so. I really should go now. Be careful,"

"You too, my son." Rose replied. "I know the way back to my room."

Exboy left his mom in the garden and returned to the computer room. Rockman was deeply focused and was watching the monitors very carefully.

"What's up?" Exboy asked.

"Nothing good," Rockman replied angrily.

"Any more problems?" Exboy asked.

"We're still rising. Don't you think that's a big enough problem to worry about?" Rockman said. "At this rate, we might land on a different planet." Rockman heard Exboy chuckle softly. "Do you think this is a joke?" Rockman demanded.

"The aliens could help us," Exboy said with a smile on the face.

"Oh sure, not only will they help us but they'll throw us a huge party too." Rockman rolled his eyes. "Are you all right my friend?" he asked.

"I don't know. What about you?" Exboy asked.

"I must be. I was the person who told you get rid of Roar before the trouble started, didn't I?" Rockman asked. Before he let Exboy answer, Rockman added angrily, "But you didn't listen, and now we're in so much trouble that we don't know what to do about it. So instead of wondering whether or not aliens could help us, why don't you think of a way to get us out of this mess."

"I think we should talk to Psychic and see if he has any solutions," Exboy said. "Maybe he will have a better understanding of the nature of Roar's power."

"Fine. Just be sure to talk to him before it's too late," Rockman said.

Psychic was playing cards when Exboy entered his room. "Can I talk to you for a minute?" Exboy asked. When Psychic nodded and put away his cards, Exboy explained everything. "What do you think we can do about this problem?" Exboy asked.

"Well, I probably should go and see him," Psychic said, so they left his room and headed towards the saving room. Psychic watched Roar sparkling throughout the room from behind the window on the door. About five minutes passed and Psychic was still staring at Roar. Exboy began losing his patience and asked Psychic what he was thinking. "Wait a minute," Psychic said. "Roar's power is colossal and incredibly complicated." He began analyzing Roar again, and after an additional silent few minutes, Psychic said, "His power acts like a combination of different powers," Psychic continued.

"Yes, I read that on the computer, but what exactly does that mean?" Exboy asked.

Psychic sighed. "It's hard to explain, but let me see if I can illustrate it for you. Fire and water are opposites, right?" Psychic asked.

"Right."

"They each have their own power. But now as far as fire is concerned, you don't want to burn yourself, right?" Psychic asked. Exboy gave a quick nod. "But if you had the power of water, what could you do with it to overcome fire?"

"Simple. I would pour the water on the fire," Exboy answered.

"Exactly, but what if they weren't separate? What if the two powers were fighting each other?" Psychic asked.

"Maybe I'd wait to see what would happen," Exboy said.

"That's a good idea in a case like this when you want to get rid of both the powers."

Psychic was about to say something else, but Exboy interrupted him saying, "I think I got it. You let one of the powers in the combination overcome the other one, and then that would leave only one power remaining. It would be weaker than before, and that would be the time to attack and destroy it."

"Exactly! You are very smart, my friend."

Exboy never liked to boast about himself, so he said, "Perhaps, but not as smart as you." Psychic laughed. "But I have another question for you," Exboy said.

"What is that?"

"Right now Roar's power is the reason why Risco keeps rising," Exboy said. "If we get rid of him, we'll plummet back to Earth and die. What can we do about that?" Exboy asked.

Psychic rubbed his chin and was silent for a few moments. "That's a good question," he said. "Give me some time to think about that."

Exboy agreed and was about to bring up a different matter when another warning stopped him. "We're landing on a planet. We're landing on a planet. We're landing on a planet."

"I have to go now," Exboy said. "I'll see you later."

"See you later," Psychic said. "I'll think about the problem," he promised as Exboy hurried down the hallway.

After punching in the necessary password, Exboy entered the computer room. "Where are we now?" Exboy asked.When Rockman didn't respond, Exboy repeated his question."I wish I knew," Rockman responded. "But is seems..."

A warning over the intercom interrupted him. "Target is found. Target is found. Target is found."

"What is that?" Exboy asked. He pointed to something standing outside Risco.

"It looks like a kid to me," Rockman said.

"A kid?" Exboy asked. "That's strange."

"It sure is," Rockman said. Rockman immediately asked for a background check on the new target. "No information matching the target," Rockman read off the monitor. Before he and Exboy could discuss the strange child further, Risco issued another warning: "Target disappeared. Target disappeared. Target disappeared."

"Where did he go?" Exboy asked.

Rockman turned around in his seat so that he could face Exboy. "I have no idea," he said. Rockman let his gaze wander as he pondered where the strange child had gone. "He must be an alien," Rockman told himself. When he brought his focus back onto Exboy, he noticed that the kid was sitting by the fax machine, playing with its buttons. "Look over there," Rockman whispered. "How did he get in the computer room?"

"Who?" Exboy asked as he turned around very quickly. Exboy saw the child and whispered back to Rockman, "Push the security button."

Rockman pushed the button in the blink of an eye, and the security alarm rang out immediately afterwards. Some of Risco's security officers entered the computer room with their guns raised, while a few guards remained by the door.

"Hands up!" one of the officers shouted. The man who had spoken was a strong and intimidating-looking officer, but the kid didn't pay attention. He acted as though he didn't hear anything. "I said, hands up!" the officer repeated again, but the kid continued to play even though all the other security guards gathered closer around him. "No strangers are allowed in the computer room," the officer insisted. "We must catch him. Now I'm only going to say this one more time. Hands up! Otherwise there's going to be trouble."

"There's going to be trouble," the alien said as he turned his head towards the officer.

"Everybody on alert and catch him," the commander said in response to the alien's words. The security guards obeyed and drew closer, ready to fire their guns if the alien showed any sign of being a threat, but when the officers touched the alien's body in their attempt to handcuff it, their hands passed through the alien's body. Stunned and afraid, they removed their hands from the alien and stepped back. "What happened?" the commander demanded.

"What happened?" the alien said, and he started playing with the fax machine again.

"Capture him," the commander ordered.

"Capture him," the alien repeated.

The commander, now very irritated and offended by the alien's words, decided to capture the alien himself. The commander had already seen what had happened with his officers' attempt, but he thought he would be able to succeed. The alien continued pushing the fax machine buttons as the commander slowly approached. When the commander touched the alien's body, his hands passed through its body just as easily as if his hand were touching air. The commander's face reddened with anger, and he went for his gun. Exboy, however, reached out and laid his hand on the commander's arm to stop him. "Sir, this is a stranger," the commander said. "He could be very dangerous. He might even be an enemy spy."

"I want you to stop," Exboy said. "We have a plan."

"Care to share the details, Sir?" the commander asked.

"I'll talk to you about it later," Exboy said. "You are dismissed." The commander acknowledged the order and sent his officers out of the computer room.

When the officers left the room and shut the door, Exboy looked at Psychic, who had entered the computer room during the commotion. He had been the one who told Exboy to stop the commander.

Exboy and Psychic looked at the alien, who was still playing with the fax machine. The two men shared a bewildered look before Exboy asked, "All right. What are you going to do now?"

"Remember when I said that you can use an enemy's power against himself?" Psychic asked.

"Yes," Exboy said hesitantly, "but I don't understand what you mean," Exboy added with an impatient tone.

"Who is your greatest enemy right now?" Psychic asked.

"Roar," Exboy answered without delay.

"Exactly," Psychic said. "But don't you think we might be able to use this alien's power against Roar?"

"Possibly, but I'm not sure," Exboy said. "First of all, how do you know the alien is stronger than Roar? And second, how do you know the alien will cooperate with us?"

"Well, it's my job to figure all that out," Psychic said. He cast a glance in the direction of the fax machine. The alien had not stopped playing with the fax machine. Psychic stared at the alien's face for a while, scrutinizing and analyzing every physical detail about the child, but the alien didn't pay any attention to him. "He is a very strange and I would guess a strong creature," Psychic finally said, when he turned back towards Exboy.

"How do you know that?" Rockman, who had silently approached the two men, asked.

"You will see," Psychic replied. "What is your name?" Psychic asked the alien.

"What is your name?" the alien asked Psychic.

Psychic faced Exboy and Rockman again. "I told you he is very strange," Psychic said. It was clear from Rockman and Exboy's expressions that they didn't understand, so Psychic turned back around to the alien and asked, "My name is Psychic, what is your name?"

"What is your name?" the alien repeated.

"You see?" Psychic said excitedly. "He repeats what I ask him."

"He does seem to be copying you," Exboy said.

"Not completely, though, just partially," Psychic said. "It's as if he only has a short term memory."

"Tell him different things and see what he says," Rockman said.

"I go to school," Psychic told the alien.

"I go to school," the alien echoed.

"I go to school at 8 'o clock every day," Psychic said.

"At 8 'o clock every day," the alien said.

Exboy chuckled. "He's like a parrot," Rockman said.

Psychic ignored Rockman's remark and began pondering over the alien's physical appearance. "His body is very different from ours," Psychic commented. "As you already saw, if you touch him your hand will go straight through him—like he was made of air. "But I believe I have some good news for you," Psychic said.

"What?" Exboy and Rockman asked together.

"His name is Binga," Psychic stated manner-of-factly. As soon the alien heard his name, he turned his head towards Psychic for a minute and said something that neither Exboy nor Rockman could understand. Nevertheless, the pair was astounded by what they had just seen and heard. They looked at each other and then looked at Psychic.

"You can speak the alien's language?" Exboy asked. "How?"

"Yes, I can speak his language. That's why they call me Psychic," Psychic responded.

Suddenly, Risco sent a new warning over the intercom: "The Target escaped. The Target escaped. The Target escaped."

All went silent in the computer room. "I have to go now," Exboy finally said, and he quickly left the computer room. Exboy rushed to check Roar's room, but when Exboy arrived, a wave of shock and panic swept over him. The first thing he noticed was that the door was slightly ajar. Exboy stood still for several minutes as he listened, waited, and tried to calm his racing heart, but he could not get over the nagging feeling that something was about to happen. Exboy clenched his fists and took a few deep breaths before he stepped forward towards the room. He moved cautiously and quietly, but when Exboy reached the door and had placed his hand on the door handle, he could go no further. Fear made his feet feel like lead. He couldn't move; he was as still as a statue. Exboy tried to look through the crack between the door and the doorframe and the window on the door when, all of a sudden, a hand grabbed his shoulder. Although Exboy was a very strong and brave young man, he froze, terrified. He couldn't even breathe.

"Who are you?" Exboy whispered after several moments. He didn't dare turn his head to see the newcomer.

"Why are you so scared? Look at me," the stranger said.

As soon as Exboy heard that, he turned around and found himself looking at a very ugly face. That face was so hideous that Exboy didn't even want t look at it.

"My name is Bikti," the unfamiliar man said. "What is your name?"

"My name is not important. How did you get in here?" Exboy demanded.

Bikti didn't reply. Instead, he laughed.

"What's so funny?" Exboy asked.

"I can go anywhere I want to," Bikti said.

"I'm going to call my Security Guards. You won't be laughing so much then," Exboy threatened.

"You can do whatever you want to, but first let me tell you something: they won't be able to capture me. Oh, and now that I think about it, it's not good manners to be rude to someone who's trying to be nice to you," Bikti said.

"So you mean you're one of those aliens?" Exboy asked.

"I sure am. Who else would I be?" Bikti asked.

"I was just making sure," Exboy said. "But if you are an alien, how are you able to understand and speak my language?" Exboy asked.

"That's a long story, but the short answer is that I've been to Earth once," Bikti answered. "I can tell you the details later," Bikti assured Exboy. He smiled and added, "By the way, were you looking for something in that room?" Bikti asked.

"That's none of your business," Exboy answered as he tried to fight his anger.

"Oh, come on, don't be so rude," Bikti said again. "You must realize how strong I am. That's why I really want to help you."

Exboy preferred keeping the matter a secret, but he thought for a little while and remembered what Psychic had told him before. With Psychic's advice still echoing in his mind, Exboy explained everything about Roar to Bikti.

When he had finished his story, Bikti was laughing again.

"What are you laughing about?" Exboy asked.

"I can't believe how serious you are when you talk about Roar," Bikti answered. "Roar is nothing compared to me. You will see."

"I hope so," Exboy said.

Bikti clapped Exboy on his back. "It has nothing to do with hope, my new friend. You can count on me."

"But we have to find him first," Exboy reminded the alien.

"You don't know where he is?" Bikti asked.

"That's the problem," Exboy said. "He used to be in that room, but now he's gone. He must have escaped." Exboy shook his head in amazement.

"But how?" Bikti asked.

"I'm not sure how," Exboy said. "The only thing I know is that when I came here, I found the door open, and Roar's energy was no longer contained in the saving panel."

Bikti listened very carefully to everything Exboy described. He could see the worry in Exboy's eyes, so he said, "Don't worry about it. We will find him."

"You'll stay with us, then?" Exboy asked.

"I most certainly will, and I will help you capture and punish Roar," Bikti promised.

Exboy felt slightly relieved by Bikti's words, so he asked the question that had been bothering him ever since he had met Bikti: "By the way, you never told me how you got in here."

"I have the ability to pass through the objects. Bikti answered simply.

"That must be the same power Binga has," Exboy whispered to himself.

As soon as Bikti heard the name Binga, his eyes widened with surprise. "Did you say Binga?" Bikti asked eagerly.

"Yes, Binga is an alien child we found in the computer room. I'm sure he's still playing with that fax machine," Exboy said.

"What a naughty boy. I've been looking for him for a long time," Bikti said. "You say he's in the computer room?" he asked.

"I would suppose so," Exboy answered.

"Could you please take me to him?" Bikti asked.

"Of course," Exboy said, and he led the way to the computer room. Psychic was still talking to Binga, so Exboy and Bikti stood quietly by the door for a few moments and listened to Psychic and Binga's conversation. Exboy didn't understand a word, but Bikti followed their exchange very closely.

"Who is your father?" Psychic asked.

"Bikti," Binga answered.

Exboy turned to Bikti in utter surprise. "What did he just say?" Exboy asked.

"Psychic asked about Binga's father and Binga said my name," Bikti said with a shrug.

"So you're his father."

"Is there anything wrong with that?" Psychic asked from his seat besides Binga.

"No, of course not. I just wanted to make sure." Exboy replied.

Rockman released an aggravated sigh. "There is nothing wrong with two people being father and son. The problem is Roar," he said. "What was the warning about, Exboy?" Rockman demanded.

"The warning was about Roar. Roar has disappeared," Exboy answered.

"What did you just say?" Rockman asked. He made no attempt to hide the fury in his voice.

"I just said Roar has disappeared," Exboy answered.

"You're so relaxed!" Rockman cried. "You act as if nothing has happened! What is wrong with you?"

"Nothing is the matter with me," Exboy shot back. "You're the one who needs to calm down, so get control of yourself, Rockman. What would you have me do?"

Before Rockman could say anything, Bikti interrupted them. "You're fighting for nothing!" he exclaimed. "You should relax and come up with a way to solve this problem. Save your energy for an arm wrestling match," Bikti added with a smile on his face.

"This it not the time for jokes Mr. Alien," Rockman said. He was still very upset by the situation and angry with Exboy, but he added, "Regardless, I could beat you at arm wrestling in the blink of an eye."

"Oh really?" Bikti smiled. "First of all, let me to introduce myself. My name is Bikti, not Mr. Alien, and second, come on! Let's see who is stronger!"

"Guys, we have more important things to do," Exboy said. "Stop arguing."

"No. I want to show him how strong I am," Rockman insisted. He and Bikti sat down at one of the computer tables so that they faced each other and began their arm wrestling match. The result came quickly. Rockman was both surprised and ashamed when in no time at all, he lost to Bikti. His astonishment and embarrassment soon turned into anger, and he refused to talk to anyone.

"Good effort," Exboy tried to assure Rockman. Meanwhile, Bikti talked to his son in their own language. He pulled him away from the fax machine, and Psychic overheard Bikti tell Binga they were leaving.

"We really need your help," Psychic said. "Allow me to show you to your rooms." He beckoned for Bikti and Binga to follow him, and together, they left the computer room.

Exboy decided to visit his mother to see if everything was still all right. When he reached her room, he knocked upon the door, but he had so many things on his mind that he was completely startled when the door opened. And yet, Exboy was even more surprised by the person who stood in the doorway. Exboy was not sure if he was awake or if he was dreaming. He rubbed his eyes, but there was no denying Exboy was definitely awake and that he was looking at the most beautiful girl he had ever seen in his life.

"Hello," the girl said.

"Hi," Exboy, who suddenly felt rather shy, replied.

"My name is Bianka."

"I'm Exboy," Exboy said a little breathlessly.

"Nice to meet you," the girl grinned.

"Nice to meet you too." Exboy's heart was now beating very fast, and a sort of energy that he couldn't explain shook Exboy's body and made a cold sweat appear on his face.

"Have you come here to see our mom?" Bianka asked.

Exboy could only nod.

Bianka giggled. "So what are you waiting for? Come on in."

Exboy entered the room and Bianka shut the door behind him. Rose was seated on the couch, but as soon as she saw her son, her heart filled with excitement and happiness. "What is going on here?" Rose asked as a large smile lit up her face.

"What do you mean?" Exboy asked.

"Who is she?" Rose asked.

"I don't know. I think you know better than I do," Exboy said.

"She says she is an alien looking for her father and her brother," Rose explained.

"What are their names?" Exboy asked Bianka.

"My father's name is Bikti, and my brother is Binga."

"Oh really? What a coincidence. You've come to the right place. They're here," Exboy said.

Bianka clapped her hands together. "Oh, that makes me so happy!" she exclaimed. "Where, where, where are they?"

Exboy laughed at her eagerness. "All right, all right," he said. "We'll go see them, but would you mind telling me who you are and how you got in here?"

Bianka explained everything. "Now you tell me who you are," she said.

"To be honest with you, we're in considerable trouble," Exboy said, and he took his turn to explain everything to Bianka.

"Oh, how dreadful! But if that is all true, I'm ready to help you," Bianka said. "Now can we please go so that I may see my father and my brother?"

Rose could hardly take in all the information that Exboy and Bianka shared. She started to ask more and more questions, but Exboy stopped her.

"Be patient, Mom," Exboy said. "I'll tell you everything later." He knew his mother would not be happy with that answer, but it would have to do for now. Exboy and Bianka left the room, but while Exboy was walking with Bianka he soon forgot about his mother and began asking himself how Bianka's father could be so ugly and Bianka so beautiful. Before Exboy found the courage to ask Bianka any questions, they arrived at Bikti's room. "Here you go," Exboy said. "This is your father's room."

"Thank you so much," Bianka said.

"Not a problem," Exboy replied. "Oh, and by the way, you know my language very well," Exboy continued.

"Thank you," Bianka said.

"Well, I better go. I've got lots of things to do," Exboy said. "See you later."

"See you," Bianka said.

Exboy made his way to the doctor's office. He was almost late for an appointment but made it just in time. When the doctor checked Exboy's foot, he grew very sad. "I'm going to have to cut the infected toe," the doctor said.

"Are you serious?" Exboy asked disappointedly.

"Yes, unfortunately I am," the doctor said. "I'm afraid there's no choice. If I don't, the infection will spread throughout your body faster."

Exboy took a deep breath and released it slowly. "Ok, go

ahead and do it," Exboy said."Remember, this is the price you pay for getting smarter and stronger," the doctor said. "The good news is the more you lose from the lower half of your body, the smarter and stronger your upper half will become."

"Until?"

"Until your energy reaches such a level that neither you nor I can imagine," the doctor answered.

"But how will the story end?" Exboy asked.

"Don't ask me such hard questions," the doctor replied. After a few silent moments, the doctor admitted, "I hope your power would win."

"One can only hope," Exboy said, and the doctor proceeded to amputate one of Exboy's toes. The doctor made the area numb, so Exboy didn't feel any pain. Exboy thought about his future as the doctor tended to the wound, and as he sat there, he realized he was feeling much stronger than before. Exboy's eye sight improved, and he could feel a mysterious power fill the muscles in his hands. Exboy was anxious to see his power develop, but he knew the process would take time.

Several days later, Rockman was still mad about losing to Bikti, and he refused to speak to anyone. Rockman's behavior irritated Exboy because he thought Rockman was acting exactly like a spoiled child.

He finally confronted Rockman and said, "What's wrong with you? You're acting like a kid."

"There's nothing wrong with me," Rockman said. "You're the one who supports a bunch of aliens."

"It's not like I don't have a good reason for supporting them," Exboy said.

"Oh? And what is your reason?" Rockman asked.

"They can help us."

"Oh yeah? How can you be so sure? How can you trust them?" Rockman asked.

Exboy paused before he said, "We have to take the chance."

"That's not a chance, that's a risk," Rockman replied.

"So what should we do?" Exboy asked.

"I don't know," Rockman answered.

"You never know anything," Exboy accused. "You're only good at arguing," Exboy added as he left the room.

While Exboy and Rockman spent their days concerned about Roar, their alien guests enjoyed comfort and relaxation. Binga could often be found sitting alone in his room blowing bubbles. Several years ago, his grandfather gave him a large, magic bubble wand as a gift. "The only person who can use the magic of this bubble wand is you—no one else," Binga's grandfather had told him. "When you just look at each bubble, a face will appear. Then you can make a wish." But there had been an exception: "If you finish your conversation with the person in the bubble before the bubble bursts, your wish will be granted. Otherwise, you'll have to keep trying. And each time you blow a bubble, a new face will appear. But each face you see will have a different level of power, depending on the size of the bubble. If the bubbles are big, a giant will appear, and his power will be greater than those on a smaller bubble."

Binga had been a very small child when he received the bubble wand, but he didn't fully understand the concept of big wishes. Binga only wanted simple things. His first wish was only to have lots of toys, so he blew some bubbles with his magic bubble wand and began staring at one of the bubbles. Sure enough, a face appeared.

"Yes Sir, what can I do for you?"

"Let me see. I want to..." Binga began, but he couldn't finish his conversation because the bubble popped. "My bubble burst!" Binga whimpered.

Ever since then, Binga rarely completed his wishes. He either took too long making his wish or something interrupted Binga's conversation. But his bad luck never seemed to bother Binga. He played with the magic bubble wand every day. Binga had even brought his bubble wand aboard Risco.

Binga preferred to play with his bubble wand when he was alone in his room. He had just started talking to one of the bubbles one day when Bikti came in and interrupted him. "What are you doing, my son?" Bikti asked.

"I'm just playing, Dad." "Playing with bubbles?" Bikti asked.

Binga nodded. Binga was not worried about his father catching him because he knew nobody could see the faces on the bubbles.

"Do you like it?" Bikti asked.

"Yes I do. The bubbles are pretty," Binga answered as the bubble burst behind him. Binga didn't get the chance to finish his conversation, but he was used to that happening. Some of the bubbles lasted longer than others, so sometimes the conversation between Binga and the face on the bubble lasted a long time before the bubble burst.

The longest conversation he ever had happened one day on Risco. Binga blew a huge bubble and stared at it. Within seconds a very large giant appeared on the bubble and greeted Binga. "Yes Sir, can I help you?" the giant asked.

"Yes. What's your name?" Binga asked.

"My name is Loo," the giant responded, "but Sir, before my bubble bursts, please tell me your wish."

Binga could not stop staring at the giant. He was huge and incredibly muscular. Binga was so amazed by Loo that he asked the giant to flex his muscles.

The giant did as he was told. Loo's muscles impressed Binga so much that he couldn't help but say, "Wow, what big muscles you have."

"Thank you, but Sir, I might burst any moment. What is your wish?" the giant asked again.

"How can I be like you?" Binga asked.

"You should exercise," the giant said. The bubble drifted above Binga's head, but he could not focus on making a wish. "Am I correct to assume you don't have a wish?" the giant sighed.

Loo's words brought Binga out of his daydreams. He tried to concentrate on coming up with a good wish. "I do have a wish," Binga said.

The giant looked a little irritated, but he asked politely, "And what is that?"

Binga considered Exboy's troubling situation. "I'm curious about the kind of problem Exboy has," Binga stated.

"Well, your father..." But the giant couldn't finish what he was about to say because the bubble popped.

Binga was shocked to hear his father mentioned. He raised his eyebrows and went into deep thought. "I wish he could have finished what he was going to say!" Binga told himself. "I don't understand what Exboy's problem has to do with my dad." Binga couldn't reach any conclusion, so he decided to blow more and more bubbles in hopes of finding the giant Loo one more time. Binga made lots of bubbles—one after another. Binga blew bubbles so fast that the whole room became full of bubbles, which were bursting one by one very quickly.

Binga tried to look at each of the bubbles. He turned his head in every direction as fast as he could, but it was useless. Different faces appeared, but none of them was Loo. Binga felt very foolish. He knew he shouldn't have wasted time. He should have taken advantage of his opportunity to make a wish as quickly as possible.

Binga was about to go crazy with all the different faces greeting him and asking what they could do to help. Binga didn't need any of them. Binga needed only one giant, but Loo was gone.

Binga kept blowing bubbles. After a few minutes, Exboy entered Binga's room. He was completely amazed by what he saw, so he asked, "Can you tell me what you're doing?" But then he remembered Binga couldn't understand his language.

"What you're doing?" Binga repeated as he looked up at Exboy.

Exboy smiled at Binga and at all the bubbles. "Children are always like that," Exboy told himself, and he left the room.

Binga was so curious and impatient about what Loo had told him that he didn't bother wondering why Exboy had visited him. Instead, he played with his magic bubble wand more than ever. Binga was determined never to waste his time again. When Loo still did not show up, Binga made a little bubble and started asking it questions about his father.

"What do you want to know about your daddy?" Binga was asked.

Time was passing by quickly. "If I knew, I wouldn't have asked you," Binga said.

"Well, you should respect your daddy, and you should listen to him."

"That's not what I'm asking. Everybody knows that," Binga said.

"Well, you should make yourself more clear then," he was told.

"Oh, I wish I could punch you in the face," Bigna pouted. He was very upset and popped the bubble himself. But Binga didn't realize that while he was talking to the face on the bubble, his father was listening to his conversation from behind the door.

Looking very angry, Bikti burst into the room. "Who were you talking to?" he yelled. His tone of voice scared Binga. Binga didn't say a word. "Answer me, Binga. Who were you talking to?" Bikti repeated.

"I...I...I was just playing," Binga stuttered.

"But you were talking about me!" Bikti insisted. Binga began shaking and couldn't say anything. A few bubbles still floated through the air. Bikti glared at the bubbles before turning his angry face towards his son's. "What do you want to know about me?" Bikti asked angrily.

"No...no...nothing," Binga answered. He was still shaking badly.

"I don't believe you. You want to know something," Bikti said. Binga remained silent. "I'm your daddy. Is there something you want to know?" Binga still kept quiet. Bikti finally cried out in frustration and grabbed Binga's bubble wand. "Until you answer my question, you will see this bubble wand again!" Bikti yelled.

Bianka suddenly rushed into the room. "Can somebody tell me what's going on in here?" she asked.

"I don't know. Ask your brother," Bikti said as he pointed to Binga with the bubble wand in his hand.

"Daddy, calm down. I know you're mad, but be reasonable. He's just a kid," Bianka pleaded.

"Kids should know how to behave too," Bikti growled.

"I know. I know, but look at him. He's so scared," Bianka said. "I promise I'll ask him about it later."

"All right, but this bubble wand stays with me in the meantime," Bikti said before he stepped out of the room. Bikti soon found a quiet place and examined the bubble wand for a while. Bikti was so curious to find out who his son was talking to that he tried making some bubbles himself. Bikti stared at the bubbles as they following each other one by one, but he was not able to see anything. "Maybe I have to say a magic word," Bikti told himself. "Abracadabra, Abracadabra, Abracadabra," Bikti repeated, but nothing appeared on the bubbles. "You must be crazy. You're playing with bubbles, and you're expecting them to talk back to you!" he scolded himself.

Someone laughed behind him. "I thought only children liked to blow bubbles," Rockman chuckled. He watched the bubbles float around the roof and laughed again.

Bikti was embarrassed and didn't know what to say. He gave Rockman an angry look and said, "I was trying to fix it."

"Oh really," Rockman said. Still chuckling to himself, he left.

Bikti was disappointed he hadn't figured out the bubble wand's trick, so he put it in his pocket and walked away.

Meanwhile, Bianka was trying to figure out what had happened between her brother and father. "I don't know! I was just playing," Binga insisted.

"Daddy says you were talking to somebody and that you were asking some questions about him. Were you doing that?" Bianka asked.

"I was just using my imagination," Binga said. He didn't want to tell the truth.

Bianka sighed and gave her brother a sympathetic look. "Oh Binga, I know you were just playing. I'll try to get the bubble wand back from Daddy," she promised. Bianka left Binga and quickly found her father. "Can I talk to you for a minute Daddy?" she asked.

"Of course," Bikti said.

"Did you know your birthday is coming?" Bianka asked.

"That's right; I almost forgot," Bikti said.

"Well, Binga and I have decided to buy you a beautiful present," Bianka stated.

"Thank you so much," Bikti replied.

Bianka looked at her father very seriously as she said, "You know what, Daddy?" Bianka prompted.

"What?"

"Children have pure hearts. Don't you agree?" Bianka asked.

"Yes, I do," Bikti agreed.

"I just wanted to remind you of that," Bianka said. She paused before adding, "Binga is a very sweet kid."

"What's your point, Bianka?" Bikti asked.

"Binga is very sad now that you've taken away his bubble wand from him," Bianka said. When Bikti did say anything, Bianka added, "The bubble wand is his favorite toy."

"So?"

"If you give it back to him, you will make him so happy," Bianka said.

"I will give it back, but he has to tell me who he was talking to first," Bikti said.

"I asked him about that," Bianka urged. "He said he was talking to somebody from his imagination. And you know how vivid Binga's imagination is, right?"

"Yes, I do," Bikti admitted. After a few minutes, Bikti gave in. "Ok, I'll give it back to him."

Bianka smiled and gave her father a kiss. "Thank you so much, Daddy," she said.

Bikti returned a smile and handed the bubble wand to Bianka. Bianka eagerly took the bubble wand and went to Binga's room.

"I've got a surprise for you," Bianka said.

"What?" Binga asked excitedly.

"Close your eyes first," Bianka said. Binga closed his eyes. "Now open your hands." Binga obeyed and Bianka placed the bubble wand in her brother's hands. "Now you can open your eyes!" As soon as Binga opened his eyes and saw his bubble wand, he started jumping up and down. He was so excited and happy he didn't know what to say.

"Oh! My bubble wand! Thank you so much! Where did you find it?" Binga asked.

"Don't worry about it. You just play with it and enjoy it," Bianka said.

"Thank you Sister. I love you," Binga said.

"You're welcome. I love you too," Bianka said, and she left her brother alone to play. Binga was so happy to get his bubble wand back that he immediately started blowing bubbles. He played with the bubble wand more than he'd ever done before.

Binga still had the question about his daddy on his mind. He played with the bubble maker for several days without seeing Loo, but one day Binga glimpsed Loo's face on one of the bubbles. "Wow, you came back again!" Binga said excitedly. "I've been looking for you for a long time."

"Hello. It is nice to see you again, my friend." Loo said. "But let's not waste time like before. Ask me your question."

"Yes, yes, yes. I don't want to waste time," Binga said. "You were telling me something about my daddy, but you didn't get a chance to finish. What were you going to tell me?"

"You have a good memory. I was going to tell you that your daddy is not your real daddy."

"What? What do you mean by that?" Binga asked.

"I hope you won't be upset with me," Loo said.

"No, I won't," Binga promised. "Now, hurry."

"Bikti is an evil creature whose name is Roar," the giant explained. "And you must be very careful around him. He is incredibly strong— stronger than you can even imagine."

"You're a liar!" Binga exclaimed. "I know my own daddy. His name is Bikti, not Roar."

"You don't understand," Loo said. "Roar has possessed your father's body, and he won't leave."

"What are you talking about? That's impossible," Binga said. He turned away but immediately spun around to face Loo again. "Can you prove it?"

Loo nodded. "Listen to me. There is a way that..." the giant began, but before he could continue, the bubble burst again.

"What bad luck. It popped again," Binga said. "How can I be sure about my daddy now?" Binga asked himself. "This is a crazy bubble wand."

Meanwhile, everyone else on Risco was taking Roar's absence very seriously. Rockman was extremely concerned about the situation and began arguing with Exboy again. "You must be crazy for allowing a bunch of aliens to help us," Rockman said.

Exboy sighed. He had heard this before. "What do you mean?" he asked.

"Guess what I saw," Rockman said.

"Just tell me," Exboy said as he sighed again.

"When I entered Bikti's room the other day, I saw him playing with bubbles. Crazy, isn't it?"

Exboy stared at Rockman and thought for a minute. "Why are you telling me this? Bikti is incredibly strong. That's why we need his help," Exboy said.

Rockman frowned. "Just remember that many things are strong, but not all of them are helpful. They could be as fatal as snake poison," Rockman said.

Before Exboy could reply, Psychic entered the room. He immediately walked over to Exboy and Rockman and whispered something in Exboy's ear. Rockman watched as a strange look come over Exboy's face while he listened to Psychic.

Exboy's eyes widened in shock. "I've got to go," he said and quickly followed Psychic through the door. Rockman watched as they left and shook his head in bewilderment. Exboy and Psychic went to Binga's room. They found him sitting in the middle of his room and looking very sad. Exboy leaned over, made sure Psychic was ready to translate, and said to Binga, "Hey Binga, how are you doing?" Binga didn't say anything. "I've been told you can help us. Will you help us, Binga?" Exboy asked.

"He sure can. He is a very smart boy," Psychic said. "Will you please tell him what you told me before?" Psychic asked Binga.

Binga had so many sad thoughts on his mind that he suddenly burst into tears

"Binga! What happened?" Exboy asked. "Did we hurt your feelings?"

"I don't want to lose my daddy," Binga cried.

Exboy glanced at Psychic before asking, "Why would you lose your daddy?"

"I don't know! That's what the giant told me!" Between muffled sobs, Binga added, "I don't have my daddy anymore. I hate him."

"Hate who?" Exboy asked.

"Giant Loo," Binga answered. He turned his tear stained face up to Exboy and Psychic and told the whole story. Psychic and Exboy listened closely. They couldn't believe what they were hearing.

When Binga finished the story, Exboy said, "You're ok Binga. Don't worry about anything."

"We'll take care of everything," Psychic said. "Don't be scared. We're going to help you." He and Exboy both thanked Binga and left the room.

On their way out, Exboy asked Psychic, "Do you believe in magic?"

"I'm not sure, but I think the boy is telling the truth," Psychic answered.

"If he really is telling the truth, then we're in big trouble," Exboy said.

"That monstrous creature is so strong," Psychic commented.

"Don't worry about it. We will destroy him," Exboy said unexpectedly.

Psychic didn't expect Exboy to sound so sure of himself. "How? What do you have in mind?" Psychic asked.

"Remember when you told me to use any kind of power to destroy an enemy?" Exboy asked.

"Yes, I did, but what do you mean?"

"You'll see," Exboy promised. "Let's go and ask Binga to show us his magic bubble wand."

"That's a good idea. Why didn't I think about that?" Psychic said.

"I just think seeing that bubble wand work will be the only way we can make sure Binga is telling the truth," Exboy said.

"I agree, but what if he doesn't want to show us?" Psychic asked.

"We'll deal with that when we come to it," Exboy responded.

When Exboy and Psychic returned to Binga's room, it was filled with bubbles. Binga stood in the middle of the room and stared at the bubbles floating around him.

"If we talk to him now, we might bother him," Psychic whispered to Exboy.

"That's ok. Talking to him and seeing his toy is more important," Exboy answered.

Psychic nodded and approached Binga. "Can we talk to you a little bit more?" Psychic asked.

Binga looked away from his bubbles and said, "Ok. You can."

"Can you show us the magic of your bubble wand?" Exboy asked.

"I really want to, but I can't," Binga answered.

"Why not?" Psychic asked.

"Because my grandpa told me that I am the only person who is able to see the faces on the bubbles," Binga explained.

Exboy thought a minute and then said, "Well, can you make a wish for something to appear? We won't need to see the faces that way," Exboy said.

Binga nodded excitedly. "You're right!" he said. "I'll try my best, but I can't promise anything because the bubble might pop before I'm done making my wish. If that happens, my wish won't come true."

"That's ok. Just try," Psychic said encouragingly.

Binga blew a bubble and stared at it for a while. A face soon showed up on the bubble and greeted Binga. "What is your wish, Sir?"

"I wish for a racecar toy, and I would like it right now," Binga wished.

"Yes, Sir." After a few seconds, a racecar appeared right in front of everyone's eyes.

Exboy was stunned and excited. "Did you see that?" Exboy asked Psychic.

"I told you the kid's honest," Psychic replied happily.

"Any more wishes?" the face on the bubble asked Binga.

"No, thank you. You can go," Binga said, and the bubble burst. "Now you see that I was not lying to you, right?" Binga asked.

"Right," Exboy and Psychic said together.

"That's absolutely amazing," Exboy said. "But now I have another question for you. Are you ready?"

"Ready," Binga replied.

"All you have to do is tell me yes or no," Exboy said.

"What do you mean?" Binga asked.

Exboy repeated himself, and Binga, still not understanding what Exboy wanted said impatiently, "Ok, yes."

Exboy laughed. "No, no. Let me ask you my question first: Will you help up with finding out the truth about your daddy?"

"I sure can help you!" Binga exclaimed.

Psychic and Exboy grinned. "Thank you so much," Exboy said.

"What can I do to help you?" Binga asked.

"What do you think?" Psychic asked. "Do you have any ideas?"

"We need to see if Bikti is my daddy. I want to surprise him and see how he reacts to the surprise."

"Do you think that'll work?" Psychic asked.

"I can't think of anything else unless I meet the giant Loo again and ask him some more questions," Binga answered.

"What do you think of the idea?" Exboy asked Psychic.

"I don't see anything wrong with it," Psychic answered.

"Ok, we will do it," Exboy said. He turned to Binga and asked, "What sort of surprise were you planning?"

Binga explained his plan, Exboy and Psychic offered a few suggestions, and they began making preparations. They arranged a huge birthday party for Bikti. Bianka helped with the party's planning and preparing. Binga, however, didn't want to let his sister know their true intentions. He knew his sister had a very sensitive heart, so he didn't dare mention anything about their father. Binga didn't like to see his sister sad, so he kept what he knew a secret.

On the day of the party, everything was set. The decorations were fabulous and elaborate. Many singers and musicians provided entertainment and excellent music. Everyone aboard Risco was invited to the party. Rose was among the guests as was Rockman, but neither of them were aware of the situation. Exboy didn't want his mother to worry, and he knew if he let Rockman in on the secret, Rockman's desperation to find and destroy Roar would mess up the plan.

Exboy and Psychic thought it best to lock the doors once all the guests had arrived. They also decided to have their strongest and best security guards surround the big party room, but Exboy and Psychic didn't mention the guards to Binga. They didn't want to risk Binga worrying about losing his father.

As the guests arrived and found their places at the large table, everyone admired the large birthday cake, which was decorated with 40 candles. Bikti was laughing rather menacingly as he greeted his guests, but he was very anxious to eat his birthday cake. Soon enough, everyone had arrived and Bikti took a seat next to the cake, but before Exboy and Psychic sat down, they made sure the doors were locked and that the security guards were in place. Once they were sure everything was ready, they found their places next to Binga and Bianka.

After a few minutes, Exboy stood up and addressed the crowd. "Attention friends! I'm thrilled you could all be here to celebrate Bikti's 40th birthday, but before we cut the cake, there are a few people who would like to say a few words." Exboy smiled and sat down.

"Happy Birthday to you. Happy Birthday to you. Happy Birthday to Roar. Happy Birthday to You."